Haunted Reflections

Part 3

Andrew Wilding

Martin and Bowman
1-855-921-1348

33 WALKING STONES

This is a story about a young woman name Princess Annie. After the events with the battle of Igworm and his minions of Iggy's and Wormy's, Princess Annie has written thirty-three sayings. Some are short and some are long. But she wrote these sayings after these battles, she wasn't born then at that time.

Here is her profile and her sayings. She is remember for all time for all of these, just like King Scarecrow, King Gobby, King Josiah, King Victor, King Iggy, etc. At the end of the day, Princess Annie is very kind at heart(on the outside) but at the same time very sad(on the inside).

PROFILE

Full Name: Annabelle Von Ada

Age: 33 years old

Height: 3 foot 10

Weight: 135 lbs

Hair: Black

Eyes: Green

Occupation: Gardener *(before she became Princess)*.

Favorite Foods: Salads, soups, bread, muffins, different kinds of berries.

Favorite Drinks: Water, tea, milk, red wine, different kinds of fruit juices.

Hobbies: Walking, reading, thinking, plays piano *(self-trained)*, plays chess.

Parents Names: Felix Von Ada-Father-Farmer, Veronica Von Ada-Mother-Housewife *(her surname was Card)*.

Housing: Before-Big cabin, lived with parents. After-Very large cottage/tree house *(Princess Annie's choice of housing)*.

EXTRAS

Princess Annie is the only child.

Never married.

Full of sadness.

Does not understand passion.

Loner.

Always dress in black(when she became Princess).

Princess Annie doesn't talk much to her parents because of her past.

The Gob-wings build her cottage/tree house.

Likes to collect leaves(she spreads them all around her cottage/tree house grounds).

Does not socialize well with others(sometimes on rare occasions).

Self taught hand-to-hand with the long sword and light as a feather while handling it.

Trains sometimes with the Mermen.

Princess Annie likes to have her own space very much most of the time.

Princess Annie has no royal blood in her nor in her family tree line, just a commoner.

Princess Annie wrote a lot of sayings which the creatures were very impressed by (maybe that is why they made her a Princess).

King Gobby's descendants royal line gave her the title Princess(the creatures insisted on it).

Out of all the sayings Princess Annie as written(around two-hundred in total),these were both hers and the creatures favorites.

This concludes Princess Annie's profile.

Now here is a list of sayings she has written
(before she became Princess Annie, a title given to her by the creatures)

1. Fallen Tears
2. Black Sheep
3. Ghost Child
4. Concrete Angel
5. Wood-Weed
6. Black Rose
7. River of Sins
8. Ship to Nowhere
9. Memories of Self-Achievements
10. Do for others-Last Eternity
11. Wings of Imagination
12. Crystal Trees
13. Urns of Freedom
14. Fistful of Tears
15. Peaceful Rivers
16. Misty Mountains
17. Haunted Minds
18. Troubled Flowers
19. More Cheer in a Graveyard

FALLEN TEARS

"Do you know why water comes down from the sky? Why it rains when the sun is out? Because the Gods up above envoy us all. They envy us because we are mortal and they are not. They can't die but we can. The Gods are jealous of us because at any given time or moment we can die and lose everything we have and own, they can't lose anything that they own or possess."

"We feel pain, sadness, grief and even feel forgotten. They can't feel that kind of things that we all feel. They cry on us all because they wish they were mortals just like us. They are eternal by there failures of the past and want us mortals to forgive them, give them redemption, a second chance but most important of all, to be remembered because they are Gods, they want to be notice, they want to fit in with us mortals as a large group, as a whole."

"Us mortals shed tears too. We cry because we feel there pain. We feel, in many different strange ways, feel sorry for them. But all I can say about the Gods up above is that they will never find what they are looking for, no matter how strong, powerful, intelligent and good-looking they are."

"At least us mortals can smile, even it is the tiniest little thing, the Gods will never smile again. They all forgot how to smile and they all try what that feeling feels...... that feeling is happiness."

Annabelle Von Ada

BLACK SHEEP

"I often ask myself this question over and over, "Why others judge another when they do not know them for who they are?", very puzzling if you ask me. If you don't fit in, don't do things to please them, in the mind..... you feel abandon or in better worlds....neglected."

"When it comes to the physical appearance, a lot of times you are judge in that manner. Wrong way for both worlds.....in what you are wearing, different hair color, too big or too small. But at the end of the day you are the same species as them. So the question is why? Why judge someone or something in that low-minded way."

"My answer is that if you have something to show for like money, for instance, you are a somebody. If you have no money than you are a nobody. If you are highly intelligent-great! But if you are low or even average intelligence-drop dead. And the list goes on....very sad I think."

"If you think you are different from everybody else, either by physical or mental, they are the ones who are different. They are the ones who need to catch hold by the hands and show them the true meaning of understanding their true nature of self-judgment and listen to there own words of what they are really saying."

Annabelle Von Ada

GHOST CHILD

"Like a slave serving a royal family, just a pair of arms and legs doing someone else's work, cleaning and cooking.....just to keep the peace for a few hours. It is like you don't even exist."

"I ask myself, "How can someone live like this, day-in and day-out? To be treated in this manner?". I think, to myself with this kind of experience, they are the ones who don't exist. They are lost with no hope at all, no common sense to mix with it and also no chance in the afterlife for peace......just nothing but pain and misery."

Annabelle Von Ada

CONCRETE ANGEL

"Such powerful beings but yet trapped by there own divine power. They watch over us all the time, when times are good or bad but when they are given a choice to pick one or the other, they can't decide so they would turn into stone or a statue."

"A lot of times I see them in graveyards. To me, they are not watching or protecting the dead or there souls for that purpose of them being there, they are place in this position because these beings are cursed, they could not make a decision if they should help others in good situations or if they where in bad situations. All I can say is that with such power they all have, you are telling me they could not make a decision with the knowledge they all have?"

Annabelle Von Ada

WOOD-WEED

"There are two differences in the word. Wood is for the dead trees that surrounds us all and Weed is for the dead weeds that cover all over the dead trees. Trees are more less people, living....breathing among us all."

" But trees and weeds don't last if you burn them. If you don't they last for an eternity. Why do they last a long time? I will tell you why. It is because they feed on the sins and guilt from others, they seem to be no stranger of it as a matter of fact."

"In time they will disappear into thin air and be forgotten like a small child letting go of his or her balloon. Or someone stealing or taking your last piece of candy from you."

"Black is for the color of the trees and green is for the color of the weeds. These colors, to me, are symbols which black is for the sins of others and green is for the guilt of which they can't live with themselves of what they have done to others and to themselves as well."

"Poor, poor Woodweed. I wonder if he or she is still alive? I very much doubt it because these trees and weeds are coming and going all the time. They don't even know they are alive."

Annabelle Von Ada

BLACK ROSE

"A rose is supposed to be a symbol of love. But if that love is broken or fake, it will change color....black! Love is very hard to find these days, I know, I have been there myself".

"There is one thing I have notice about roses is that they are protected , they are deceiving by there looks and beauty. They have thorns on them like soldiers protecting there kingdom when danger is coming. When the thorns cut you, they take the blood and keep it for themselves because it is a reminder to the thorns that you tried to take an advantage on them".

"When they change color, they remind themselves how cruel the world is because others are judging roses by there looks and beauty, not by there soul and intelligence".

"All I can say about a rose is that when it changes color, run, because when there thorns strikes at you, you can't haul them out plus you will be curse for all eternity into no hope in finding true love, no soul mate to spend to rest of your life with".

Annabelle Von Ada

RIVER OF SINS

"If there is a river out there that would dry out soon, I would very much like to know what that river is. But I know of a river that will run for eternity and that river is very much alive and won't be dry as a bone anytime soon. The sins of others keep this river flowing, sometimes very slow and yet sometimes very fast too".

"I wonder if this river ever did stop did stop, taking a breather, flowing through the sins of others, inside them I mean. If it ever did, I myself would be sinless or am I sinless? I guess the only sins I have to myself I guess is attacking at others by giving my own personal opinion and what I really feel about that situation......is that a sin?".

Annabelle Von Ada

SHIP TO NOWHERE

"I was never on a ship but others told me it is a nice experience. They told me it feels like you are free as a bird, the skies the limit, no turning back to reality......just very peaceful and no issues to complain about".

"If there is a ship like that? If there is I would really like to go for a ride in that ship. The only ship I heard and have been on aboard is the one that takes you to the endless open body of nothing, no world around you, no color, no beauty, no nothing".

"I guess I am wrong for the first time in my life, there is a ship like that, the one others told me about........ in there own minds, of course".

Annabelle Von Ada

MEMORIES OF SELF-ACHIEVEMENTS

"I have mastered my very own accomplishments and that is sadness. Yes, I did and very proud of it as well. Others think of me as different but I look at them in a different way too".

Here is a small list of my self-achievements of sadness.

Sorrow
Grief
Alone
Forsaken
Used
Taking Advantage
No appreciation from others
Being Forgotten
Neglected
No Friends
No family to call my own
Extra arms and legs to please others
Abandon
No help to call upon
Being hated by others for no apparent reason
Smacked Around

"At least the creatures understand what I went through because they have experience the same ordeal of sadness. After all, I did say it is a small list, didn't I? Or should I add more to the list?".

Annabelle Von Ada

DO FOR OTHERS-LAST ETERNITY

"Guilt is one of the most fastest aging remedies alive. This is something I am very good at, no, highly experience at it. That is doing deeds for others who don't appreciate it at all what-so-ever".

"The thing is that if you help someone in need and just say that person wrong you a few days ago, the guilt on that particular other at that moment would eat him or her alive because the very one who helped him or her in need....that stays with him or her in the back of there own coincidence forever.....in there own mind".

"What goes around, comes back around.....I love it and the best part of all you don't have to do a thing. But there is one thing that I did do or should I say use to do to others(in the past)is that I would actually sit down and force them(in the mind)to talk in an actual conversation in which they didn't want to do. I was a good talker..... really good indeed".

"One thing is for certain and it is an one hundred percent factor, to me that is, there is always time to think before you actually get to feel guilty after words. A lesson learned the hard way.....I know".

"At the end of the day, when I look back at this, I felt guilty at times. Was I going down the same road or path as they were...feeling guilty? I hope not".

Annabelle Von Ada

WINGS OF IMAGINATION

"The fantastic thing in the whole wide world is, to me, is the world of imagination. No one, living or breathing, can tell you what to do....only you can tell yourself what to do. You are the leader who leads in a world which can be anything and the outcome from your own actions....the skies the limit".

"Getting these wings is something you have to earn the hard way...in the mind. I tell you all now, when you do acquire these wings, you will look back at what you have accomplished and say to yourself at the end of the day is that if I have been given such a powerful gift received from a higher place, then to me that is a blessing which I will have for all eternity and a high privileged to be given this gift by whoever".

"For the record, these wings should be used for good purposes, not the evil purposes. I ask yourself, "Why would anyone, in the right mind, use these wings of imagination for evil?". Maybe it is me but I will never understand that til the day I die".

Annabelle Von Ada

CRYSTAL TREES

"I find trees very innocent looking and yet at the same time they can cause a lot of damage, even it is towards others or themselves. I ask myself over and over again, "Why others attack the innocent for no reason?". Just because they are at ease enjoying nature or is it because they blend in very well?".

"I guess if they were made of a different element besides wood, I would have to pick crystal. You can't burn or destroy them easily, not like wood. But with crystal there beauty would last a lot longer, keep there figure perfect, no wind to blow or cut them down, not even fire can't burn them either".

"But the good points of real trees is that animals can live in them, make there homes inside and outside of them. Plus insects can do the same thing with real trees".

"Crystal trees, to my personal opinion, are like beings from above, they are perfect but nothing lasts forever. Even these trees can fall down like the real ones......if you know the right element to do so, of course".

Annabelle Von Ada

URNS OF FREEDOM

"I notice something that I know too well.....that is people, creatures, the Mermen and I guess if there are other species out there go through hardship times. I know, I have been there myself more than once".

"The peace that everybody would like to have is something that they would never get, in there own minds, of course. That is when the body dies, feels no pain at all, both physical or mental. Every time I see urns, I see freedom".

"The urns, to me, are a symbol of peace. These bodies can't come back to life because they are ash, not like a body buried. Even though I am a true believer of urns, the escape route path of a different realm. I ask myself, "Is there any kind of freedom of there?". I guess you have to urn it first".

Annabelle Von Ada

FISTFUL OF TEARS

"My hands are weapons, a tool, a sign, a marker and also a helper. But they are no use when they are full of tears".

"The tears that others let go, run down on there faces are more powerful than anything I have experienced. Tears are mixed with happiness, joy, sadness, anger, left alone and the list goes on. But when you get a handful of them, they are like weapons, a tool, a sign, a marker and a helper(in the mind of others)".

"Tears.....are they good or bad? Which one overpowers the other overall? I often ask this question to myself many times and the only answer I get is ....Hope".

Annabelle Von Ada

PEACEFUL RIVERS

"When I am hurt both physically and mentally, I would normally walk down and sit by a river, watch the water run down the stream for hours and hours. I find rivers very peacefully, especially in the mind.....relaxation and totally free from everything....like reality".

"I guess that is where the souls go, after they leave the body. They go into the rivers.....the streams of peace, freedom from everything until they are judge by them. Maybe that is why I feel peace and free, maybe my soul is already there, myself waiting to be judge and given a new life. Is my old self in the afterlife and my new soul is the one I have?".

"When I look at rivers now I see coffins.....flowing down the river banks on a journey to the afterlife, all of them going and waiting to be judge by whoever. The rivers are not blue, they are black, like the night sky without stars......can see the blue only when the moonlight is shining on the water and the stars twinkling in the night sky, guiding the souls to there freedom....no physical or mental pain".

"One thing I can say about the rivers now is that they, to me, look very sad. If the rivers had a chance for a new life, would they pick or choose a new life? My answer is no because they are the guardians of souls and the souls ease there pain and suffering(the rivers that is)".

Annabelle Von Ada

MISTY MOUNTAINS

"Wonder why the mountains are always covered in a foggy, cloudy, whitey appearance all the time. I think it is because the souls from the planet were trying to be with the Gods from above but the Gods won't let them in their realm".

"They try very hard to enter but the highest point that they all can reach is the very tops of the mountains. Poor Misty(is who I call the leader of the mountains because the mountains looks like a mist in a long distance)tried very hard to enter the Gods realm with all the souls power. But that is just my belief but in reality I think at times, maybe, their is really something there because the mountains are always covered in a cloud. I think Misty was a powerful leader in the afterlife but that is just my opinion".

"Why would the souls want to be in a realm with the Gods while they look at us from above and wish they were mortal? There must be reason for them to get out of that realm. Too much responsibility or maybe they are sick of the divine power. Who knows but one thing is certain, the mountains are a symbol from the Gods above and that symbol is unhappiness and wish they could join the souls surrounding the mountain tops".

"All I can say to Misty is that if you can reach the realm of the Gods, you are in worse shape than ever which you can't break the chains of madness".

Annabelle Von Ada

HAUNTED MINDS

"We are all haunted by what we see and what we do....bad deeds that is. Not necessarily bad, at times we all witness a lot of things we see not by what we do and see it through our own eyes".

"I am haunted for sure. I often wonder why others treated me wrong. For example, when I am gardening, not just my own gardening for my parents but most of the time for others, it wasn't good enough. Digging up plants and replanting them, painting, weeding, cutting the grass, cleaning out their green house and placing everything back the way it was before".

"If I am haunted.....for sure they are haunted too because the only explanation for all of this is that they are the ones who likes to be haunted. If they haunt others with their past faults, they are addicted to that ingredient.....very sad in my books".

Annabelle Von Ada

TROUBLED FLOWERS

"Very beautiful these living species they are indeed. They can fit any occasion like weddings, funerals, hospitals or just to give to a loved one. I never had anyone give me any flowers, I wonder what is must feel or be like for someone to present you with flowers".

"I look at flowers and feel sorry for them. They can't walk, they stay in one area or in one spot all the time. This is just an educational guess but I think the more of a beautiful species there is(could be human, creature or plant)the more cursed they are because others jealously on beauty makes beauty die quick and turns to weeds".

Annabelle Von Ada

MORE CHEER IN A GRAVEYARD

"So true that a graveyard is more happier than the living. They feel no pain, no suffering and yes, no one to be bullied upon".

"I find it really relaxing in a graveyard, just like a river flowing down the stream with the wind blowing through your hair. I can hear a lot of laughter in graveyards, almost like a celebration or party or even a dance surrounded by a very large group of people, creatures or even Mermen for that matter. I envy them at times but I am here....alive and breathing. Trying to find my real purpose of this life I have going for me".

"I say to myself, "What would it be like to be a graveyard worker?". I think I would rather have like that kind of job because, to me, I am helping or releasing their souls from their bodies so they can find peace and harmony. If I could myself and be free from pain and suffering, I would but maybe I am buried. Maybe I am in a graveyard.......looking for peace and harmony......like everyone else out".

Annabelle Von Ada

GRAVE DIGGERS

"What an honorable species they are. Fantastic warriors, great workers but at the end of the day....they are all dead.....not one exists. They were created to please others and not themselves....not right at all".

"First, according to the history books, King Scarecrow created and named them so he could fight against King Luke. Second, Queen Sandra made a doll that looked like a Grave Digger and gave it to Igworm. Lastly, Igworm drop the doll on the ground near the gates at the Kingdom of Hydra. The doll came to life, started to dig into the ground and up came thousands of Grave Diggers to fight against Igworm and his minions which came from the ground as well".

"I wonder what it would be like if they were alive today. I wonder if they have feelings or a soul for that matter. Did they all have that sort of thing? Did they really enjoy what they did in the past? I often ask myself that question over and over again in the back of my head".

"One thing is for sure they are remembered and not forgotten. The Mermen made a statute of a Grave Digger at the keep where King Scarecrow and King Iggy lived. I wonder if I will be remembered? Will I? Or am I another Grave Digger doing someone's deeds in disguise that I really have no idea about? I guess time will tell but a lot of that time I feel I am a Grave Digger but at the same time I feel I am something else".

Annabelle Von Ada

HYDRA

"I often wonder why the Mermen name this country Hydra. Maybe because there is a beast-like-creature in the past that the Mermen discovered and didn't tell anyone about. Maybe the Mermen look after the Hydra in the past and it is still alive now. Or maybe because the Mermen wanted to feel protected(in their own minds)that a creature such as that existed".

"The Mermen have been around for a very long time. I have no idea how many years or centuries they have walk these lands or others lands to be exact. They have been around a lot, traveled everywhere but they never name any other place they have settled but here.....to what I have learned. Why Hydra and why these lands? Is there a beast out there? If so.....where? In the mountains where the Mermen settle? In the water? In the sky? The word Hydra, to me, stand for a certain meaning, just the same way of thinking as the Mermen, I guess. Here is my theory".

~H: High and Mighty
~Y: Yarns and Livestock
~D: Dunes and Habitat
~R: Rivers and Freedom
~A: Alone and Happy

"And again it is just a theory but I was wrong before in my life.....about a lot of things".

Annabelle Von Ada

MAZE FOR LOVE

"I am always in a maze looking for a soul mate but that maze is very tricky and very hard to complete by finding your way out of there. Some parts of that maze is easy and some are dangerous".

"I have to accept the fact their might not be anyone out there for me but if King Scarecrow were alive, myself and him would be a perfect match. Myself and King Scarecrow have so much in common. Every time I enter that maze, I was hoping to find King Scarecrow but again, this particular maze is one huge jigsaw puzzle. I am not the only one alive looking for that perfect soul mate".

"I guess some mazes, in the mind, can be easy to get out but everyone is different. Am I different from everybody else alive?".

Annabelle Von Ada

FLAME OF CREATION

"The Flame of Creation.....what a weapon to have at hand created by the souls by the creatures in the afterlife. A blessing and yet at the same time very deadly and dangerous too".

"My personal opinion I don't think I am worthy of such a weapon but yet I really believe the Flame of Creation had a certain meaning for its figure. This is my theory and only a theory....for the record".

~F: Fury
~L: Living
~A: Anger
~M: Mighty
~E: Eternal

~C: Creature
~R: Rise
~E: Earth
~A: Army
~T: Timing
~I: Ideas
~O: Overboard(numbers)
~N: Nature

"Deep down in my sad, black heart that I have, if the Flame of Creation was not created, would their be a King Scarecrow present? Would their be a country of Hydra? Would their be creatures living among humans and the Mermen? I as myself if there is a power in the afterlife to create something as powerful as this particular weapon, is their a power among us living, breathing beings that live among us and yet to be discovered by a chosen one to use?".

Annabelle Von Ada

SAP OF LIFE

"When I see sap on trees.....I see life. For example, if an insect is covered in sap and hardens that insect all over, preserved for many years and later take the blood from the insect and make new life, like the Flame of Creation.... for example by making the Grave Diggers. The creatures said it can be done by the sap but I never have seen it happen first hand but it would be very interesting".

"I think about the sap more and more. By the end of everything which is lay down on the table....about the sap on the trees, maybe the sap can bring something back from the dead. Look at the trees, for example, are they alive? Are they breathing? Are they not a type of species that live among us all? Yes! They are. If that was the case, the past would no longer by a past but a walking past among us all.....almost like history coming back to life and telling us all about the events in the past from the actual heroes and heroines....word for word....think about it".

Annabelle Von Ada

PRETENDERS OR COWARDS?

"I ask myself this question a lot, "What makes others pretenders and cowards? Or one or the other?". I was never neither but I was surrounded by both of these types....very sad indeed".

"Are pretenders cowards or are cowards pretenders? I think, to me, are mixed of both because pretenders are the fake version of themselves and let their guard down like cowards. Also cowards are the weaklings who attack the innocent but at the same time pretend, in their own minds, they are doing the right thing in that situation".

"Overall, my answer to both pretenders and cow-ards.....very weak souls and curse by past souls who have sin in the past. Or are they weak and cursed together from the past and even now? Either way, to my own opinion with experience......it is very sad, senseless and pathetic".

Annabelle Von Ada

ARE PEOPLE OR WHOEVER AGAINST YOU?

"I don't think people or different kinds of species are against you. I think they are attacking themselves of what they all went through in their lives and that is just my opinion but I was wrong before".

"What I have learned about others is that I see a lot of pain in their faces and eyes. I look at them and see only misery and their only remedy to cure that pain(in their own mind)is to attack others with their own sadness. If they are unhappy, why would they try their very best to make you unhappy? Make you feel like a nobody? To even their own odds to their personal life, they wanted to let everyone around them be on the same level, the same ship they are on route with the wind blowing very hard into no stopping, no turning back either. I guess King Scarecrow must have felt the same way".

Annabelle Von Ada

OPEN FIELDS OR BUTTERFLIES?

"Such a hard decision to make....both at peace and harmony".

"The open fields.........they are wide open where the wind can blow through them and relaxing the minds of each piece of grass on the ground, no one to bother them, no one to walk over them.....just nice sunny days, starry nights to look at and rain to get a drink of water(and if they want company, others cut the grass and children play as well)".

"The butterflies.......such freedom, such beauty and can go and do whatever they please. No worries, no troubles and no one to bother them too".

"The question is.......are the open fields and butterflies really happy and free? To me, it must be pretty boring and dull with no one to talk to different, just the same old company. My answer is that both of them are afraid of the unknown, afraid of what is out there. I guess some things in life are just too good too be true....don't you think?".

Annabelle Von Ada

WHICH IS MORE BEAUTIFUL-BODY OR SOUL?

"Some say the body is beautiful while others say the soul is. And sometimes others say both are. I ask myself which is more powerful in beauty".

"I have my own opinions about both and others have their own reasons but I ask myself the body and soul are two different things. The body may be harmed and loved by those around you but both as one can change the world by their decisions they make in the eyes of others. The soul on the other hand is a tool, fuel by faith and controlled by a higher power which has rules of how to control it".

"Which is more beautiful? The answer is......both and neither, you can't just pick one over the other. And again that is just my opinion, I am not an expert.......for my part they are link together as one, they are both living in the same field.....is it not?".

Annabelle Von Ada

SHOOTING STARS

"Whenever I see a shooting star I see a soldier, a servant and a gardener, cast out to where the Gods live. The Gods do this to them either by two reasons. One is the Gods cast them out so they can experience what it would feel to be mortal, throwing them out of their realm and when they fall, they shoot through the night sky like a ball of light. Second, the soldiers, servants and gardeners complain to the Gods because they would like to be mortal and not live forever".

"I ask myself, as a mortal, "Why would the Gods do this? Why would they like to be a mortal?". They have everything they want. No pain and suffering, lots of food, drink and clothing. Yes, even power too".

"Or maybe it is a sign from them. Maybe they are letting us know they were once a mortal and found a power on the planet for them to be Gods. I look at it this way....at the end of the day, would I choose to be a God? My answer is no because there is no challenge to it, it is not earn the right way at all. But as a mortal, you have to earn that challenge. Others say they pity the weak but I pity the power because there is no meaning to it. Very senseless if you ask me".

Annabelle Von Ada

LOST WOODS

"I have to say that this is my favorite part of this country. Well experienced and yet powerful plus at peace but at th same time full of sadness, anger and forgotten".

"It all started right here when King Scarecrow met the group of creatures for the very first time along with King Josiah(back then he was a prince). One thing I don't understand about Lost Woods is that white tree covered in large red bulbs of flowers which the creatures later called Cherry Blossom. The other trees look dead and gloomy but that particular tree really stand out the most....full of life".

"I think that white tree was a walking, talking tree of the past and when it died of old age, the creatures or the Mermen of both buried him or her there. Again just an educational guess but this country is old and wise. Maybe this is a sign for the creatures and Mermen from an unknown extinct species long ago. Maybe the creatures name this wooded realm bunch of trees Lost Woods because they are lost in this part of this world and it happen to be in these woods. Or maybe the Mermen have something there growing and it is only a matter of time it will rise, who knows for sure".

"These are just theories to me but all I can say about Lost Woods is that these woods are not dumb neither stupid. They are planing something".

Annabelle Von Ada

SIGNS OF LIGHT

"I have seen the light a long time ago but the light at the time was different. It look like a guardian angel. Yes, I saw the light in beams in the sky breaking through the clouds, in dark areas in Lost Woods. Some are big and some are small beams breaking through the dead gloomy trees but this guardian angel just stood there....leaning on a group of books in my small bedroom".

"He or she look so beautiful. I went over to touch the angel and my fingers just went through it, like air..... could not feel it at all. I think it is a message and that message is, in my mind, there is freedom and a new beginning for myself down the road. This old life will disappear, I will start a brand new life and I just only hope and pray it is a good one indeed".

Annabelle Von Ada

LOST SOULS

"My belief as a living, breathing individual....all of us all have a purpose in life....not bad but good. We all have a reason to live, we just have to get out there and find it for ourselves".

"Humans, creatures, Mermen or whatever will be lost for eternity if they can't find their reason for living. The souls of each individual have a limit, some are small while others are huge like royalty, for example. I look at others around me now and all I see is lost souls....very confused, very puzzled, full of rage and anger, depress looking and afraid of the unknown".

"Right now I am a lost soul but I really don't think I am going to be lost forever. To me, if that individual can't find their true purpose in life, their soul will be doom forever for all eternity. They will wonder in the afterlife and try to find its purpose there and if they can't find it, their soul will dissolve into thin air and enter another living, breathing specie from the same species from the old one or should I say be reborn. For example, if a human being can't find the purpose in their life or in the afterlife, that soul will enter a human being(born again just different facial features)".

"I hope I find my true purpose in my life, I really don't want my soul to dissolve or as a matter of fact....be forgotten for all eternity".

Annabelle Von Ada

OUR FAREWELL......

"Violins........pianos........harps.......cellos........
flutes.......glued inside my head for reasons which is beyond my understanding of why such music exists around
me. Maybe it is because we live in an imperfect world, full
of mindless sinners who's sole job to bring others down to
their level in life(or in better terms in their world)".

"We all try to bring peace with ourselves.....if it is at
your workplace, place of living, the environment to where
you are surrounded by others close to you. Or maybe that
special place which only you know about and no one else
doesn't know it even exists".

"When I think about life .....my life in general.....all
I see is one big fantasy world. What I mean by this is that
when things are rough, times are harsh and uneasy......I
enter a world into which I have created. That world is
called Carnival Crowns. Why this name? Easy! Because life
should be just nothing but fast rides, games, and balloons.
The rides.....some are small, others are huge. Just like life....
the rides depends on that particular individual who is rid-
ing them. The games.......test ones knowledge and patience
to show how strong you really are. Or wanting you to
participate in their own entertainment, just to fit in to ease
some tension(ease your mind from others into not harm-
ing you mentally). The balloons.....full of air.....I think not.
Full of blood......yes! Why blood? Here is my answer. In life
we all bleed....if it is by physical or mental. To escape that
atmosphere(for the moment)we think of our own escape
and the balloons can rise up, lift us from the ground and

take you to new horizons to unimaginable worlds. When the balloons brakes, the sinners pore their own blood all over you. Why? Really to blame others for their faults in life and trying to take away freedoms and escapes from others".

"But in time, as life makes you older each year, eventually you will forget the world you have created in your own mind and in this case....Carnival Crowns. I will turn into dust, six feet under.....in a ground which will have no memory, just another body resting for a re-praise, sleeping until someone wakes you up from your long slumber in the coffin which has no meaning of the one who made it. I mind as well say good-bye to this amusement park full of lost souls who enjoy the moment and only that ......in respect to them because they are letting me know I am not the only one out there thinking, living and overall hurting of what horrors we all live through..... could be tiny, small, medium, or as big as the sun".

"I say farewell to..........or farewell........me, myself and I. I know now I will never jump out of my body and have a one-on-one conversation with myself in any given time. It would be nice......but ......only one question that makes sense the most to me(I guess) and that is, "How can you stand being part of me for all these years?", which is a fair question, if you ask me. And the only response I will get is, "I had no choice, you are part of me and I am part of you. I have to live with it......that's life and plus it doesn't make both of us perfect". All I can say is that it is fair.....whichever way you look at it......really".

Annabelle Von Ada

CAWING OUT ALL STONES

"I made a necklace for myself, made out of stones.......thirty-three to be exact. Each stone has a tale to tell and only I know the story behind each one too. I should know because I have lived through them all, both in my own hollow mind and in reality. Hopefully at the end of this dark path I will find my true courage and confidence to break this necklace hanging around my neck and become something more....like an angel, perhaps".

"At first I thought it was cute to create something like this necklace but a little too late at the end though. These walking stones that I have personally walked through and a total reminder which is around my neck showing myself how unfair life can be and to make it more interesting.....I have decided to make a story out of them all, thirty-three stones of interest with thin threads of hope along with huge amounts of memory which will never be forgotten at all anytime soon. Before I describe each saying for each stone, each saying will be an adventure of a world of fantasy, fable, folklore and fiction plus at the same time very more less real both in the mind and physical matter too, to make things a little interesting for anyone to read and see(in there own mind). Thirty-three different sceneries with no picture frame to hold them all hold on a wall.....just an image from one poor soul who is looking back into the past, living in the present and planning for the future in hopes that the outcome with either break me and make me.....lets continue, shall we? Of course, I will have my best friend by my side-the long sword-if anyone or whatever decides to be brave and tower over myself in anyway possible. Thirty-three battles in my own mind really. It should be a riot and with a few laughs to go with it too.....ha!"

"One-by-one I fought each stone which were a crow. After each defeat a small bright blue beam of light came out of each one of them, releasing information from that particular crow from where they came from-the stone-telling us all what kind of life I have lived and what my mind has created to feel that I am not alone in this looking world too".

"Victory......no! With every small beam coming out from these vowel creatures who prey in the cornfields to tease the guardian there-the scarecrow-form a new specie like no other, there true identity the crows revealed to-wards myself. Standing right in front of me is a half skeleton and half human.....happens to look like me. It is me. But why? Because in order to be free from these stones once and for all to rid these nightmares that have haunted myself for sixteen years(really four years and up, can't remember below that, ha!)".

"I don't know what to make out of this.......thing. And I am not taking any chances either. This Annabelle was also armed with a long sword too. With a quick movement I run towards her and to my surprise she dodge my attack. Sword-on-sword, fight-after-fight, time-against-time, an all out war between us both until one of us makes a mistake. So I decided to use my mind to defeat this other Annabelle here. I pretended I have given up to lower her sword and for that very split moment, I quickly

slice her throat and dead in an blink of an eye........silly me,
I should have thought of this sooner. Upon her defeat,
the body lying on the ground turn to crows and no more
Annabelle. As for each saying goes, all thirty-three in
total with a few extras to add in as well, should shed some
light on how I really feel and hopefully find the answers to
what I am looking for. Enjoy!"

Annabelle Von Ada

FINAL THOUGHTS ON EACH SAYING

"Here is my personal definition on each saying but everyone else is entitled to their own conclusion. And again I am just one person and this is just my experiences I believe what I see with my very own eyes, so I apologize if anyone out there who does not agree with me. I am entitled to my freedom of speech and I believe this is a good opportunity to say what I really think about each saying. Hope you enjoy them as much as I do......I should.....I live through them".

Annabelle Von Ada

FALLEN TEARS

Sadness is everywhere. We all fall down in life but it is the courage that picks us all up and continue on the path which leads us into the unknown lands

BLACK SHEEP

To be the very one that stands out the most and trying your very best to fit it, judging you on how you live, looks, intelligence, etc. Everyone in life have favorites and you are the favorite of your own world......remember that

GHOST CHILD

Others may see right through you but only you know what gifts you have. When you share them in the world of man, they will soon recognize you and see that you are more than a somebody and not a nobody either

CONCRETE ANGEL

An angel......the gift to heal any illness of any kind. But they could not heal themselves into how to make decisions on the one they were watching over their shoulders for years. Sometimes even the powerful have a weak spot and this is one of them

WOOD-WOOD

Weeding out the weeds, woods surrounded by wood. If anyone out there in the world would tell me different that these two elements does not mix well, I am more than willing to turn this idea and dig up another because, to me, they both have so much in common.....life that is

BLACK ROSE

My favorite colors are black and red. Why? Easy! Because the thorns on the rose have black hearts and drink blood from those who take advantage on others. Of course, you can dye them in different colors like hiding their true nature around others.........that is the idea.....for some species

RIVER OF SINS

The ideal place for the sins of man and woman to be placed. Water represents evil(in dreams)and the very birth place of any kind of act of sin committed in the world. And yes, my sins are there as well. I am not perfect but my gardening tools are. I would simply tell others the opposite on how to plant or grow different plants and trees. Am I killing these living species just to get back at others for mistreating me? A sin which is a little too late, I think

SHIP TO NOWHERE

It doesn't matter where you are in life, you are always on aboard a ship. What I mean is that you are always traveling, trying to find your purpose in life. A continuous voyage from one port to another and you always end up at the same docks........lifeless action......gloomy shadows.....rotten smells of decaying fish

MEMORIES OF SELF-ACHIEVEMENTS

Everyone in life has achieve something worth their while in their life. Could be good or bad. But most of the time it is the terrible teacher who teaches you how life can be(the hard way). And it all depends on that individual who walks and collects the most experience

DO FOR OTHERS-LAST ETERNITY

I really don't understand when others do not appreciate a helping hand. Almost as if they all expect it from you(in a way). It is over my head but the guilt will kill them in the long run. Selfish and greedy......taking an advantage on a poor bystander

WINGS OF IMAGINATION

Endless flying......endless journeys......endless boundaries. These golden wings have no limit in the world of fantasy, fable, folklore and fiction. A real blessing to have when you acquire such a gift from a higher place. To me, it is very hard to describe an explanation into how anyone can write stories off the top of their head and only they know what to write down, no one else does not......I know......I am a writer and at times a poet......thank-you

CRYSTAL TREES

It does not matter what it is in life, everything has a weakness. If there were such a thing as these growing on this planet......the only thing that would cut them down.......no love! Crystal is pure, so is love(of what I heard). Makes sense!

URNS OF FREEDOM

Ashes to ashes, dust to dust. Whatever you earn in life is just a moment, you can't take it with you in the afterlife. Some may be free but others is a complete madness. Why? Because a lot of times they are afraid to where the road will take them......to others it is a tunnel

FISTFUL OF TEARS

Water........very powerful in the eyes of others. Especially exiting out of the eyes and rolling down the face. Later hitting the ground giving Mother Nature some experience and insight into how this world really feels about.....making fists into taking action

PEACEFUL RIVERS

By nature.........yes! But in your own mind.....always! One question which I find hard to answer.......and that question is......, "Are they really at peace and full of laughter? Or are they just in streams of ongoing unanswerable questions flowing on a continuous journey?". Looks are very deceiving and at the same time very cautious into where it is at

MISTY MOUNTAINS

Dew on the grounds at the mountain top ranges, mist resting at low altitudes just above elevation at any given point from the surface. Like a ghost or a group trying to find their way around for salvation. In the end...... no luck! Just their on sadness to guide them

HAUNTED MINDS

Everybody in life, doesn't matter what walk of life you are from or what path takes you, encounters troubling events or images which will stay with you til the day you die. The mind is a powerful tool......the starting process that never dies

TROUBLED FLOWERS

Is it fair.....no! But it is what it is I guess. Beautiful.....yes! Troubled.......both yes and no. It depends
how you look at this picture, really! If it is a yes than
the looks will have them rooted out of the grounds to
please others. And if it is a no than stuck in one place
when death creeps up on them and starts to wither away,
no moisture at all, dry as a bone, falling apart with no
hope coming to save them all

MORE CHEER IN A GRAVEYARD

In the common world, R.I.P. which stands for
Rest In Peace. But in my very own terminology stands
for Restless Into Pieces. Happy? Overjoyed? Full-out
party? Maybe! But if I was dead and just be on their
shoes for about five minutes.....would I feel the same
way as them? No! Why? Because my mind would be so
confused and wondering how to stop this world form
spinning in all directions

GRAVE DIGGERS

A dig for a grave while a grave is a memory for the
dig. In life different species die.....it is just a matter of
how and when it happens in life. The headstone is just for
looks and to tell others who is buried there. On the other

hand, the Grave Diggers no longer exist because of someone else's greed for power. But now they all redeem themselves into fighting on the right side of power. Today, I
only see a shovel being controlled by someone who makes
a living off it. Rest in peace my dear Grave Diggers

HYDRA

A symbol meaning water, according to the Mermen. Could mean giant, guardian, god or even maybe a
living dragon......who knows! But out of all the names to
name a country. Why this name? The Mermen are not
dumb or naive. They are very collective when it comes to
knowledge about history......and this is just one of them.
I wonder what this Hydra really looks like? I would love
to see one but in the world of brainstorming.....any image
has many possibilities

MAZE FOR LOVE

A fairy tale......nothing more and nothing less. To
me, if there were an item to travel through time....would
that make a difference? I don't think so. Why? Because it
is only you know when you are ready, no one else does
not. Even with courage and confidence mixed together.......it is a rejection from the other. Like, for example,
eating food....you may enjoy it but at the end, does not
agree with your body system internal. The same thing for

love, would it agree with me? Or not? I will never know and I am fine with that

FLAME OF CREATION

It was created to save lives but in the end it only cause nothing but havoc, heartache and misery. In a sense, at the same time, it did bring everyone back to-gether.....human beings, creatures and the Mermen. One thing I do not understand about this sword....why make it so powerful in the afterlife and let a living being use it? With such power as powerful as this sword, it would go to anyone's head. Or did it? I wonder if it happen to King Scarecrow(in his mind at least)transform him? Poor Queen Sandra.....or was it her all along?

SAP OF LIFE

Like a tree crying for help, hoping for any living specie to get glued in all around by this sticky substance. A tree is very much alive just like anyone else on this planet. Makes perfect sense when you think about the sap on trees, trapping a specie and preserving it for many, many years down the road. Like a chain.....lock one link to another to keep the life span alive

PRETENDERS OR COWARDS?

There is no shortage of these two special kinds of mixed breeds on this planet....that is for sure indeed. One is a pure two-face and the other is afraid to take on a challenge in life. Very sad and at the same time very scared because in time the truth might reveal itself out in the world for everyone to see and hear

ARE PEOPLE OR WHOEVER AGAINST YOU?

This is my meaning, "No one is against you, they are for themselves", which makes the most perfect sense if you ask myself. Someone in life going through hardship(or more than one)and decides to take as many as he or she can......to even the level of their self-pleasing, mind-thinking and simple-minding world that surrounds him or her

OPEN FIELDS OR BUTTERFLIES?

These two have something in common.....the wind! They are both open like butter just like flies out in the fields when the wind gently breeze right through them to pick them up or even glide their way a little faster, easier and more efficient either in the air or on the ground....... makes no difference if you ask me. I guess it all depends how you look at it

WHICH IS MORE BEAUTIFUL-BODY OR SOUL?

I am very curious if the question came up into the public and just listen to the responses form every individual out there. Just like being a fly on a wall, in the corners and taking in all the juicy information.....collecting and analyze each little piece of this different element, filtering out all the garage and getting the final results. Which one overpowers the other......more less......alive......which is first.....and last in the afterlife

SHOOTING STARS

Why live a life as a mortal? Challenges? To be tested by a higher power? Or by others living on the same path as you? Here is my reason and just one to solve this little riddle or game. I truly believe it is to feel alive for the first time in their lives and actually say to themselves.....thank-you..... appreciate yourself and myself.......to live, love and laugh

LOST WOODS

You can take it in two worlds......one is you are lost in the woods and two is the woods is lost out into this gloomy world of ours. We are all lost in our lives....trying to figure out which path to take to exit out from these woods. Maybe that is way this Cherry Blossom is there..... Lost Woods is nowhere to be found

SIGNS OF LIGHT

It can blind you, show you the way out, help you read, write, think, work but most importantly a message from above into a realm of great power. Blessing and the very gift when the light shines on you.....I know..... because this light shine on me. Right now I have enter into the world of literature.......rare and a mystery.....thank-you very much to whoever and I promise this gift will not go to waste

LOST SOULS

Even when different species out there alive....... human beings, creature, the Mermen or whatever is out there alive and yet to be discovered are lost after they have discover their gift which only they know how to use. My conclusion on this little mystery of mixed puzzle pieces trying to fit in as one......scared of the unknown, afraid of their own surroundings and selfish into abusing unused talent(or talents)to share with the world

OUR FAREWELL.......

Solitude.........is what I call this little act of partnership of self-imprisonment. Myself does not want to be part of me. Is it my fault? I guess! Who is to blame but only myself. After all, I am living this life or is it the ones who has placed me in this situation.........as a gardener, cleaner and a part-time cook. I have to be honest with myself for the first time in my life......I love myself but I also love gardening too. But I truly believe deep down in my sad, dark heart that I am something special. For example, writing, a rare gift to have and I hate it to see it go to waste like garbage. Until than, my other half has left me til my gift takes off and that gift is writing into the world of literature. That day will come......I know it......I believe it.......I feel it.......everyday in my sad bones and mind. In the past I hated writing and literature, now I am writing and reading.....go figure! I go by this saying for myself, "It is a dream but that was not a dream but a dream that which came true", pretty catchy I think

Annabelle Von Ada

SHORTER VERSION OF EACH SAYING

Fallen Tears: Sadness!
Black Sheep: Neglected!
Ghost Child: Forgotten!
Concrete Angel: Lost!
Wood-Weed: Helping Hand!
Black Rose: No Love
River of Sins: Guilt!
Ship to Nowhere: Discovery!
Memories of Self-Achievements: Pleasing!
Do for others-Last Eternity: No Harm!
Wings of Imagination: The Skies The Limit
Crystal Trees: Protection!
Urns of Freedom: Peace!
Fistful of Tears: Hurt!
Peaceful Rivers: Rest!
Misty Mountains: Determination!
Haunted Minds: Experience!
Troubled Flowers: Trapped!
More cheer in a Graveyard: Freedom!
Grave Diggers: Used or No Luck!
Hydra: Guardian!
Maze for Love: Finding True Love or Soul Mate!
Flame of Creation: Revenge!
Sap of Life: New Born!
Pretenders or Cowards?: Troubled!
Are people or whoever against you?: Mind!
Open Fields or Butterflies?: Fear!

Which is more beautiful-Body or Soul?: Decision Making!
Shooting Stars: Research!
Lost Woods: New Species?
Signs of Light: Hope!
Lost Souls: Exploring a new World!
Our Farewell......: A New Beginning!

Annabelle Von Ada

FINAL MESSAGE

"It was a dark and stormy night, thunder crashing into the sky above, the raining falling hard plus the wind blowing very hard as well. The creatures came to my parents home on a Tuesday, at 7:45 p.m. at night. There had to be at least ten of them in total and they wanted to speak with me. They said to me they were giving me the title princess, a symbol for all creatures because of my sayings I have written(I am very private about my personal things but I let some of the creatures read my sayings). They have spoken to the royal family of King Gobby and told them about me and what I have written. I say farewell to Annabelle Von Ada, I am Princess Annie now. What an honor it is to be a guardian of the creatures. My parents are happy for me(I guess they are)and I say good-bye to this old life and say hello to my new life".

All my love, Princess Annie, Guardian of the Creatures

CREATURES OF THE WILD

"I would like to personally thank the family of King Gobby's decedents in a bloodline of honor, valor and leadership who gave myself the title princess. To be honest and truthful I really had second thoughts of not accepting this honorable title. I was half-on scared at first but when I collected myself upstairs in my head where my mind lives, you creatures and myself have so much in common......like these thirty-three sayings. Or is sayings something new to you creatures? Like I understand your pain in life where there are different species are around and all but.........maybe finding an answer you creatures were looking for all these years. I never thought it would give myself a title, let alone be this important to you creatures........thank-you......from all my mind, strength, body, heart, blood, soul and faith, I am grateful and a deep gratitude from you all. I will serve you all well to the best of my ability and hopefully lead to a great acceptance, security and respect. At first, to be honest with you all, it will be hard to adjust but should pay off in the long run.........I hope........for myself and for your sake too".

Princess Annie

CROWNING SOME PUZZLES

Crown-
Won+Now/Crow+Row/Cow+Corn/Roc+Con/Won/Now

"When I see my crown resting on a pillow in my quarters, I see ten words come out. What do they all mean? Here is a list of each definition for each pair and maybe.......just maybe......find the answers to what I or we were looking for."

> **OWN+NOW-possession and moment**
> **CROW+ROW-birds in groups and lining up**
> **for battle**
> **COW+CORN-milk and grain for everyday living**
> **ROC+CON-ancient bird and never taking orders**
> **from anyone**
> **WON+NOW-victory and life-time moment**

"A symbol, a status, a giant mean one thing for myself and that is a tower or a guardian, whichever way you want to place either one, really. Looking down on the innocent and depending on myself to protect them now and later down the road. It is funny when I think about my childhood, my very past......no one never protected me, not even one creature for that matter. And now they want me to protect them........go figure, indeed. It is a nice gesture by having one but I will never wear it. Not because of selfishness but out of guilt......not mine but there guilt. Fancy this and fancy that-jewels, emeralds, rubies and diamonds-no shortage of that but to myself.......it all comes down to looking and feeling important. Sad but true but this is just how I feel......how I really feel about this crown sleeping in my bedroom. Good-night and rest in peace my dear crown."~

Princess Annie

IF ONLY I COULD.........

".......turn back time to see a different me, would it be fair?"

".......sit down and listen to myself for just once in my life."

".......gain the confidence and move on out into the
        unknown."

".......find the courage in the past and escape the issues
        at hand."

".......seek my inner mind sooner and create a product
        like no other."

".......power up my own strength to conquer anything
        around myself."

".......build my body hard enough to defeat any evil
        out there."

".......break a heart and if only anyone out there could feel
        the way I feel."

".......boil the blood within myself to let everything out of
        how it really feels".

".......suck the soul out of my body and see how it looks for
        future purposes."

".......bank any faith and sin without harm-good luck with
        that I say."

".......walk along side by myself and just feel the feeling of
        company."

".......sleep away and never return to reality, enter a realm
        of peace."

".......drink something different and feel the effects from it,
        a good effect."

".......write down every single issue and read back all of
        them-a reminder on life and myself."

"......place myself outside of myself, sit down and just
        watch-mistakes replace by credits."
"......mirror myself and see the real truth for just once and
give my mind a rest and ease some satisfaction to let myself know where I stand in this life of mine. But the truth
is revealed to myself as I sit in this huge tree house/cot-
tage palace of mine, up in my quarters, build by the Gob-
wings who I am so proud of. And that truth is becoming
a princess. Am I happy? I guess so. All I wanted is acquire
my very own shop and sell different kinds of flowers and
create new ways to improve a healthier lifestyle for myself and for others around. It is what it is at the end of the
day.......maybe I should take up writing. After all, the creatures now do all my gardening for me...............thanks."

Princess Annie

IT ALL STARTED WITH.........

"......a piece of paper, a feather-pen and a small vile of ink".

"......collecting life all around myself".

"......a shovel and a wheel barrel".

"......the very first tear rolling down my face".

"......an issue which never really rested for years".

"......the very first accusation on myself and completely
        innocent at the end".

"......riddles and puzzles".

"......just a simple prayer to Jehovah at a tender age of four".

"......a pair of rubber boots and gloves".

"......micro-brain species dance and sing over the rich who
        are not really rich-sad".

"......having a conversation with one creature-go figure".

"......the cold silence with just myself to entertain".

"......a doll who was always there for myself and happen to
        secure any problem-thank you".

"......an older man who said to me, "You will never go any
        where in life". At first but never the last".

"......my very first tree climb in an unknown wooded realm".

"......music to my ears and listening to there pain".

"......a window, looking out but never in. What I mean
is that looking forward into the future and never ever
looking back at all. Seeing the light at the end of the tunnel, in this case, the window is wide open. Never closed,
never locked and no shades blocking out the sun either.
In my life I just had a few cracks down the road in the
past but eventually healed up in time. If it were ever
smash into many pieces of glass, the afterlife would be

my new home. Glass is a reflection on my life and a window would be the best choice to be part of my life. I have to say for the record, it all started with............accepting who I really am and never change for anyone even if I have to lose something so dear to me........oh..........but I have lost something in the past.......my lovely rock wall I personally made........pity".

Princess Annie

SIXTEEN PHASES IN LIFE

Guarding your grounds!
Arming yourself for the right protection!
Resting both mind and body, more energy to press
forward with!
Dirt goes with the territory, get use to it!
Evening with a cool breeze to escape reality!
Never quitting and never backing down from a task
given to you!
Forward and never backward, no freedom that
way!
Over the valley and in the distance is the true path
to take-the unknown!
Right direction means pointing in the right
direction!
Open up one door and discover the full truth for
yourself!
Number yourself as two because to get to number
one will be your soul mate!
Endless numbers means endless choices to take-
you make them, no one else!
Security to never be poor but to live comfortably!
Ever responsible to keep going and staying alive!
Leaving your old self and discovering your new
self!
Free yourself and only than you will be truly be
that you did by pleasing yourself and not others!

"Like climbing hilltops, weeding your way up to reach the peak of glory and yet still weeds up there that need major weeding, In definition, meaning that is doesn't matter how much praise and security you have, you are bound to have troubles down the road. Many times it is the long path you take, nine chances out of ten it is that and mostly never a short path either. Another example is a shadow, planting a tree in the evening when the sun is going down to rest for completing a hard days work on the grounds, not just seeing your shadow but the new born tree-the shadow-letting you know you have save a life from dying or even death at your very own palms covered in dirt and wet soil. Really life needs to be weeded out everyday of the year......that is a fact. I know I am still doing this job and I am a princess.......even high status are not so lucky there days, don't you agree"?

Princess Annie

LIFE'S DIRECTIVES

Like a shadow lurking in the darkness, just waiting for the right moment to strike at you very hard and sudden, not holding back either. Just the fallen tears that land on us all when the rain is out, giving Mother Nature something to drink, wash and clean. So can the black sheep can give something back like in a hope of sense change his or her coat from black to white. Does not want to vanish like a ghost child into nothing.......trying to make a name for itself. Down the road it would be such a waste for any kind of talent go unused like a concrete angel who lost it all by decisions he or she could not decide on.

Around every corner, there are gloomy trees but not necessary trees in general but human beings, creatures, the Mermen and yes even wood-weed too. Still standing......dead......leaving its mark for all to see.......even the black rose stand tall with not a single soul to haul her up from the ground to be presented by anyone around. Just a noise in the background......a stream......ignoring the standings of the haunted memories of the dead of bark wood and neglected flowers, the river of sins, where others go in for a swim to baptism themselves to take away their sins for all eternity.

Open body of water, in dreams water means evil and their voyage for a non-meaning purpose for a ship to nowhere who is just wasting the wind and the sails time. I guess the only good thing out of this is your memories of self-achievements which will be glued inside your books and later in life read them back to catch up on some old times.

Innocent as they are, innocent as they come around, we as individuals do for others-last eternity. And what I mean by this is the guilt others have to live with, the very ones who wrong you and the task that was completed by are the victims who are the ones they trusted the duty to fulfill......the sinners. I can only imagine how they are feeling, thinking or even believing that such acts would come back and bite them, haunt them or better yet destroy them.

Now you can't forgot the sky for which what they have to offer. Like an open book with blank pages waiting to be written in, waiting for a new owner to acquire the wings of imagination to take him or her beyond any quest. The skies the limit......taking flight until these wings need a well deserve rest. Thank the heavens for these crystal trees close by, this new owner needs to energize the batteries for these golden wings.

The living keeps on flowing while the dead comes to pass. It is very significant for these urns of freedom to finally get the peace and freedom that they so rightfully deserve. Even going to a graveyard sometimes you can't hold back your very own fistful of tears. And not just there but anywhere in life in general. When hope, courage and confidence is not on your side......your hands are now a fist......trying to open them like peaceful rivers to free yourself from your prison of pain. While in time your hands are loose as a feather......gliding freely into the sky til it reaches misty mountains, resting at the very peak of this very stronghold of a kingdom for which no man has any chance to reach this particular goal of a quest elsewhere.

Coffins......made out of wood most of the time and on rare occasions made out of stainless steel. Headstones...... some are polish and some are not. Being trap inside one of these hand made tools no wonder these poor souls have haunted minds, even the dead can feel this......pretty much as if still alive experiencing this. Resting on these boxes are the troubled flowers who sole job is pleasing the dead at this moment and at this given time of space and atmosphere. In a sense you can feel it....really. There is more cheer in a graveyard escaping reality of the living and now going down the long tunnel into the reality of the afterlife. The only company allow in the graveyard for this huge celebration are the scarecrow looking species.....the grave diggers.....which is only fair for their part. Because they are the only ones who actually care for them both alive at their grave and in the realm of the dead with a lantern lighting in the darkness to show them the way out.

Entering a maze made out of plants from the heart of Mother Nature.....which can only mean one thing.....and that is very obvious into what this is. Treasure? No! Power? No! But the guardian of this maze knows exactly what it is. Half dragon and have fish, this hydra will go to certain lengths to protect the heart of the core in this old ancient labyrinth where bones are scatter all over the ground into which quite a few hopefuls tried their very best to reach their goal. All of their courage, wisdom and strength could not acquire the maze for love which is the prize. It stands for true love and finding that particular soul mate with this power.....like a needle in a haystack.....as such.

The flame of creation ....a weapon like no other around and can finally rest in peace for all eternity for it too can't even control its own destiny for which it has no control over the hourglass of time. If I was this particular powerful sword would I create life or destroy it. In this case it was both. At the time from the beginning..... for evil. In the end.....for the better of a greater cause. A sword like no other and never be another one like it of its kind either.

The element of wood.......a tree......which can do wonders for any living specie alive out there. You can build from them, make fire to help others out, a fantasy item children call them a tree house which is directly on the tree. But if the sap of life made from the trees could harden precious memories......I bet I would in an instinct. There is also the down point for these trees falling down, they are a living specie which are cut off the life span to help others out. In order to do this act they would have to kill them to make any kind of progress to move forward. Are they pretenders or cowards? Into why place your face into a two-face act and pretend it is okay to cut them down for pleasure or just attack at them with a blade or a torch for they can't walk nor run away from a situation that went wrong. I ask myself this question over and over again trying to make some sense into it for which maybe is it just me, "Are people or whoever against you?", is something like fishing, for example, you fish out the fish and just lay them there on the ground to die....not make any use out of them. The same goes for trees....why cut them down and make no use for they are there for a purpose. Are they that much of a negative eye sore for every-one to see? The ones who attack are really the eye sore in the public eye.

Without this element, this planet would be one big open ruin for all......the sun. It is like if life can survive without it....I think not. For example, can life live with open fields or butterflies? Or in better English simple terms, "Can life live without a clear open mind or chal-lenges?". Another example would be, "Which is more beautiful-Body or Soul?". Or again in simple English terms, "Is speech more beautiful than faith?". Everyone has their own beliefs and questionable answers for them-selves or out to others for that matter.

Looking up at the night sky, for instance, you might be lucky enough to see a rainstorm of shooting stars go-ing in all directions. Traveling at speeds trying to match its competitor....the light. But on the ground level to catch all the action, trying not to miss this amazing moment of a lifetime. Up in the front seat is our white covered red flower bulb friend who the creatures name Cherry Blos-som.....Lost Woods. Bringing some life to this lost part of the world.....the gloomy kingdom........darkness into hid-ing.....with no hope for any signs of light. Why? Because these abandon old trees are afraid fo the light and if it did shine any light on them.....would they feel happy or scared? Both.....really. Happy in a sense someone or something recognize them for who they are and scared if they all forgot how to socialize because they haven't seen anyone for years.....maybe centuries for the record. Maybe one day these lost short, small, tall, huge wooden species will have their time but for now these trees are having a time of their lives.....the night sky in their sight of endless music.....the eternal sonata.....sings in their minds and soul.

Light and darkness........darkness and light.....both are the enemies for lost souls but at the same time are the allies for these sad looking two-legged unidentified souls. Light blinds them but helps them see the way out into a new direction to take. Darkness confuses and blinds them all around but helps shelter from nearby creatures of the night. It is how you look at it actually. Eventually, these souls will find their way home to a new home. Until than, I say farewell.....our farewell.....to each single one out there and never forget I will be thinking about you all because I used to be lost......a soul at one time soulless but still had one.....on a road with no map to guide me and no one for a helping hand either. I call this short story.......Life's Directives......because this is what life brought to myself and my decisions both reality and fantasy, along with fable, folklore and fiction too. Good-bye for now and remember just one thing......you are not alone in both worlds.

Princess Annie

To Be Continued.......